OTHER TITLES IN
THE RAILWAY SERIES

The Three Railway Engines

Thomas the Tank Engine

James the Red Engine

Tank Engine Thomas Again

Troublesome Engines

Henry the Green Engine

Toby the Tram Engine

Gordon the Big Engine

Edward the Blue Engine

Really Useful Engines

Percy the Small Engine

The Eight Famous Engines

Duck and the Diesel Engine

More About Thomas the
Tank Engine

More About
Thomas the Tank Engine

CHRISTOPHER AWDRY

WITH ILLUSTRATIONS BY
CLIVE SPONG

HEINEMANN YOUNG BOOKS

More About Thomas and the Tank Engine

Originally published in Great Britain 1986 as Book 30 in The Railway Series
First published in this new edition 1999
by Egmont Children's Books Limited
239 Kensington High Street, London W8 6SA
Book design by Mandy Norman and Traffika

ISBN 0 434 80463 0

1 3 5 7 9 10 8 6 4 2

Printed and bound in Italy

DEAR FRIENDS,

Sometimes Thomas and Percy both think they are the most important engine on the Branch Line. We know better, of course, and so does the Fat Controller, which is why he did not intervene when Thomas and Percy had a quarrel. Like most quarrels, it wasn't serious to start with – it began when Percy … But why not turn the page and then you can read about it for yourself.

THE AUTHOR

Thomas, Percy and the Coal

Thomas the Tank Engine's blue paint sparkled in the sunshine as he puffed happily along his branch line with Annie and Clarabel.

"Blue is the proper colour for an engine," he boasted to the other engines.

"Oh, I don't know, I like my brown paint," said Toby.

"I've always been green. I wouldn't want to be any other colour either," added Percy.

"Blue is the only colour for a Really Useful Engine –
everybody knows that," spluttered Thomas.

Percy said no more. He just grinned at Toby,
and winked.

Each day Percy brings a truck full of coal from the Junction, for the coal merchants at Ffarquhar. Next morning Thomas was resting when Percy arrived.

"Be careful in this siding, Percy," warned Thomas, as Percy pushed the trucks along the line beside him. "These buffers aren't very safe, they …"

He got no further. As one of the coal trucks passed Thomas, the catch on its door burst open. With a rumble and a crash an avalanche of coal poured out and piled up around Thomas' wheels.

A thick cloud of coaldust arose all round him.

"Atishooo!" spluttered Thomas. "Help, I'm choking!
Get me out!"

Percy looked worried. Then, as the dust settled, he looked at Thomas and began to laugh. Thomas' smart blue paint was black from smokebox to bunker.

"Ha, ha, ha," chuckled Percy. "You don't look Really Useful now. You should see yourself. You look Really Disgraceful."

"I am *not* disgraceful," choked Thomas furiously.

"You did that on purpose, Percy. Now stop your stupid giggling and get me out."

But it was some time before Percy could help.

The coal-bunker stood behind the buffers which Thomas had said were unsafe. It was only when the coal was shovelled into the bunker that Thomas could be moved.

Poor Thomas was filthy.

"You're not fit to be seen," grumbled the cleaners.

It took so long to clean Thomas that he wasn't ready in time for his next train, and Toby had to take Annie and Clarabel with Henrietta. The cleaners were tired and dirty when they had finished.

Thomas was grumpy in the Shed that night. Toby thought it a great joke, but Percy was annoyed with Thomas for thinking that he had made his paint black on purpose.

"Who'd have thought it?" Percy remarked. "Fancy, a Really Useful blue engine like Thomas becoming a disgrace to the Fat Controller's Railway."

"You wait, Percy," replied Thomas crossly. "One day you'll laugh on the other side of your smokebox."

"Pooh!" rejoined Percy. "I wouldn't have missed all that fun for anything."

The feud worsened as time went on. Thomas thought Percy had coal-dusted him deliberately, and Percy was cross with Thomas for thinking so.

Two days later Thomas was at the platform when Percy brought his trucks from the Junction. Percy arranged them and ran into a siding for a drink before Thomas' train left.

The water-column stood at the end of the siding with the faulty buffers. As Percy tried to stop he heard a cracking sound and to his horror found that he couldn't.

The buffers didn't stop him either.

"Ooooer!" wailed Percy. "Help!"

The buffers broke and Percy ran into the coal-bunker with a thud. Coal flew everywhere, and when the dust had settled Percy had disappeared beneath a thick black cloak.

Thomas watched from the platform. As the crash died away, the signal-arm dropped and Thomas moved off, laughing as he went. Percy was furious and he spent the rest of the day wondering how to pay Thomas out.

 # The Runaway

P ercy was soon mended, but one morning Thomas woke feeling ill. The Fat Controller sent him to the Big Station to see if they could make him better there, but it was no use.

"Edward must take you to the Works," the Fat Controller told him.

Then he went to see Duck.

"I want you to go and help Percy and Toby while

Thomas is ill," he said. "Donald and Douglas will do your work here until Thomas comes back."

Duck was delighted. He knew Percy already, and it wasn't long before he had made friends with Toby, Terence and Bertie. Percy, who was still cross with Thomas, was glad to have someone new to talk to.

Even Annie and Clarabel were impressed.

"Such nice manners," they told each other. "It really is a pleasure to go out with him."

They soon made Duck welcome, and he laughed when they told him how Thomas had once left their guard behind at the Junction.

When Thomas
came back Annie
and Clarabel told
him how well
Duck had
managed.
Though Thomas
was jealous at
first, he was so
pleased to be home
that he soon forgot it.

But he didn't forget the affair with the coal. Percy was careful to keep out of his way.

The Works had left Thomas' handbrake very stiff. It made his brakes seem as if they were on, when, in fact, they weren't, and Thomas' Driver and Fireman soon learnt to be extra careful.

But one day Thomas' Fireman was ill, and a relief man took his place. At the Junction, Thomas ran round Annie and Clarabel. While his Driver chatted to the Stationmaster on the platform, the Fireman fastened the coupling. The Driver had told him about Thomas' brake, but unluckily he had forgotten. When he had finished with the coupling he joined the Driver and Stationmaster on the platform.

Thomas simmered happily. In the distance Henry appeared.

"Not long now," thought Thomas.

At that moment Thomas felt his wheels begin to move. He tried to stop, but he couldn't without his Driver and Fireman. He tried to whistle a warning, but he couldn't do that either.

The Guard shouted from the platform, but that did no good. The Guard, Driver and the Fireman were all stranded, and the passengers were left on the platform staring. Thomas, Annie and Clarabel gathered speed out of the station. The empty coaches shrieked as they rounded the curve, but Thomas, with plenty of steam, kept on going.

The Signalman at the Junction soon realised what had happened, and sent a message along the line. An Inspector prepared to stop the runaway at the station near the airfield where Harold the Helicopter stood ready in case of emergency.

But Thomas was still going much too fast. Quickly the Inspector climbed aboard Harold and they took off.

"I must get there in time, I must," he whirred anxiously.

Below, Thomas was tiring.

"I need to stop, I need to stop," he panted wearily.

Annie and Clarabel held back as they went uphill. As they neared the station, Thomas saw Harold land and the Inspector run towards the platform, where he stood waiting. This time Thomas entered the station slowly enough for the Inspector to act. Running beside the train, he judged his moment, jumped and scrambled into Thomas' cab. Then he put the brake hard on.

With a sigh of relief, Thomas stopped.

The Inspector mopped his brow.

"Phew!" he remarked.

Wearily, Thomas agreed with him.

Better Late than Never

Workmen were mending the viaduct on the main line. The arches needed strengthening, but the Fat Controller did not want to close the Railway while the work was done, and so repairs took a long time. The engines had to take great care when crossing the viaduct, and the delay often made them late at the Junction. Thomas was cross.

"Time's time," he grumbled. "Why should I keep my passengers waiting while Henry and James dawdle about all day on viaducts?"

"Don't blame me," snorted Henry one day. "If we hurried across the viaduct it might collapse, and then you'd have no passengers at all. What would you do then, eh?"

"Run my trains on time, for one thing," retorted Thomas, and hurried away before Henry could answer.

At the Top Station
Bertie was timed to
arrive just after
Thomas. His
passengers soon
found that instead
of going straight
from Bertie to their
train, they were
having to wait until
Thomas arrived.

"Late again," remarked Bertie one day, as Thomas
panted wearily in, ten minutes after time. "I thought you

could go fast, Thomas. It's time we had another race – I reckon I could beat you now."

Thomas went bluer than ever, and let off steam loudly.

"Rubbish!" he hissed fiercely. "I'd still beat you any day. It's those main line engines. They dither about on their viaduct and then blame the Fat Controller's workmen. It's just an excuse for laziness, if you ask me."

One day James was later than ever at the Junction.

"I'm sorry, Thomas," he puffed, as he came
breathlessly to the platform. "I was held up at the Big
Station, and the viaduct made it worse."

"It's lucky for you I'm a guaranteed connection," snorted Thomas. He puffed importantly away, leaving James at a loss for words.

"Peep, peep," whistled Thomas at every station. "Get in quickly, please."

The passengers did their best, but Thomas soon found that he couldn't save much time.

As they neared the tunnel, Thomas thought he saw a flash of red on the road beside the line.

"That looks like Bertie," he said to himself, "but Bertie should have got to Ffarquhar ages ago."

"It *was* Bertie. Thomas stopped as close by as he could.

"What's the matter?"
he asked.

"I feel dreadful,"
mourned Bertie.
"All upset inside,
and Driver says
he can't make me
better. Thank
goodness you're late. Can
you take my passengers, please – they'll never get
home otherwise."

"Of course," agreed Thomas.

Thankfully the passengers climbed into Annie and Clarabel, and after promising Bertie that he would send for help from the next station, Thomas set off again. Already he was feeling much more cheerful.

All the passengers reached home safely, and when Bertie was better he came to thank Thomas.

"I'm sorry I teased you about being late," he said.

"That's all right," said Thomas. "I'm glad I could help. Perhaps being late isn't such a bad thing after all."

Drip-Tank

One evening Percy was bringing empty stone-trucks from the harbour. He was tired of his quarrel with Thomas, and wanted to be friends again. He had had a good day, and was feeling extra pleased with himself. He was so busy thinking how he would tell Thomas and Toby about his expert handling of the trucks that he forgot to keep a good look-out.

Too late he saw a broken branch hanging over the line straight in front of him.

"Oooooer," he groaned.

He tried to stop, but his brakes wouldn't hold him.

"Ouch!" he exclaimed a moment later. The branch hit his smokebox, broke away and crashed to the ground.

Percy was more startled than hurt, but his front was still sore when he reached the Shed.

"It's your own fault," said Thomas, unsympathetically. "You should keep a better look-out – I've no patience with you."

"Pooh!"

retorted Percy huffily. He forgot his good resolution and talked to Toby for the rest of the evening.

Percy didn't speak to Thomas the next day either.

"I say, Toby," he said in the Shed that evening, "what's a drip, do you know?"

Toby pondered.

"It's when rain comes through a hole in your cab, and Fireman hasn't got time to mend it," he decided at last.

"That's silly," objected Percy. "I heard a boy on the platform call his friend one this afternoon. I'm sure *he* couldn't have come through a hole in my cab," he added earnestly.

Thomas was tired of being ignored.

"That's different," he interrupted loftily. "The boy just thought his friend was being a coward, or silly, or a spoilsport." Percy thought about this.

"So if …" he suggested reflectively, "… if you stopped me from doing something nice, would you be a drip, Thomas?"

"You're the drip," answered Thomas crossly. "Now go to sleep like a sensible engine and stop talking nonsense."

Percy was offended. Instead of going to sleep he became even more determined to pay Thomas out.

Next day Henry's train was late at the Junction. When Thomas set out along the valley he was trying to make up for lost time.

Suddenly there was a loud bang, and something hard hit the bottom of his left-hand watertank.

"Ouch!" exclaimed Thomas, and stopped. As he did so he felt water splashing cold against his wheels.

"One of your siderods has broken," said his driver. "It swung up and punctured your tank – we'll have to get help."

At Ffarquhar, Percy was shunting. The Stationmaster came up.

"Leave those trucks please, Percy," he said. "Thomas has got a hole in his watertank — there's water dripping everywhere, and he can't get home on his own."

Percy was still cross with Thomas.

"I won't go", he said. "Thomas called me a drip — let him jolly well stay there and drip himself."

"But what about Annie and Clarabel and the passengers?" reminded Percy's Driver. "Do they deserve to stay out all night too?"

Percy was sorry at once.

"I forgot them," he said.
"We must rescue them
in case they turn into
drips too."

He hurried away.

He found Thomas
near the river. Everyone
was glad to see him, and
the passengers thanked him
for coming.

"I'm sorry I was rude," said Thomas, as Percy helped him back to the Shed. "That tank of mine turned me into a bigger drip than we expected, didn't it? Can we be friends again, please?"

Percy was delighted to agree.